S0-AKZ-528

DREW BREES

BY MARTY GITLIN

Published by ABDO Publishing Company, 8000 West 78th Street, Edina, Minnesota 55439. Copyright © 2011 by Abdo Consulting Group, Inc. International copyrights reserved in all countries. No part of this book may be reproduced in any form without written permission from the publisher. SportsZone™ is a trademark and logo of ABDO Publishing Company.

Printed in the United States of America,
North Mankato, Minnesota
112010
012011

Editor: Chrös McDougall
Copy Editor: Sue Freese
Interior Design and Production: Christa Schneider
Cover Design: Craig Hinton

Photo Credits: Winslow Townson/AP Images, cover; Michael Dwyer /AP Images, 4; Kathy Willens /AP Images, 7; Tony Gutierrez /AP Images, 9; Michael Conroy /AP Images, 10; Paul Sancya /AP Images, 12; Tom Strattman/AP Images, 15; Lenny Ignelzi /AP Images, 16; Denis Poroy /AP Images, 19; Robert E. Klein/AP Images, 20; Ed Zurga /AP Images, 22; Bill Haber /AP Images, 25; Paul Abell/AP Images, 26; Mark J. Terrill/AP Images, 29

Library of Congress Cataloging-in-Publication Data
Gitlin, Marty.
  Drew Brees : Super Bowl champ / by Marty Gitlin.
    p. cm. — (Playmakers)
  ISBN 978-1-61714-743-2
  1. Brees, Drew, 1979—Juvenile literature. 2. Football players—United States—Biography—Juvenile literature. 3. Quarterbacks (Football)—United States—Biography—Juvenile literature. 4. New Orleans Saints (Football team)—Juvenile literature. 5. Super Bowl—Juvenile literature. I. Title.
  GV939.B695G57 2011
  796.332092—dc22
  [B]
                            2010046215

TABLE OF CONTENTS

Drew Brees

CHAPTER 1

FAMILY AND FOOTBALL

Growing up, Drew Brees often visited his grandparents. He and his other young relatives sat on the grandparents' porch and ate plums. Then they took turns spitting the plum pits as far as they could into the yard. Whoever sent the pits flying the farthest was named the winner.

The Brees family loved to compete in any way they could. That desire helped Drew become a star quarterback in the National Football League (NFL).

Drew Brees was a competitive person long before he was a star quarterback for the New Orleans Saints.

Drew was born on January 15, 1979, in Austin, Texas. Austin is the capital of Texas, where the favorite sport is football. Drew's younger brother, Reid, was born two years later.

Drew's parents were Mina and Chip. They got a divorce when Drew was seven years old. This upset him very much, and he often cried himself to sleep. But it also helped Drew and Reid become closer.

Drew and Reid were as much friends as they were brothers. They spent hours tossing around a football in the tiny yard outside their home. Sometimes they tried to run the ball past each other for touchdowns. Drew often got down on his knees and tried to tackle Reid as he ran by.

The Brees family had a strong sports background. Chip had played college basketball. Mina was a three-sport star in high school. She ran track and also played volleyball and basketball.

As kids, Drew and Reid Brees made money by fishing golf balls out of a nearby creek that ran through a golf course. The brothers cleaned up the balls and sold them to golfers. Then the boys used the money to buy baseball cards and bubble gum.

Family has always been important to Drew. He and his wife Brittany now have their own son, Baylen.

Her brother played quarterback at the University of Texas. Her father was one of the most successful high school football coaches in Texas history. Drew and Reid handed out water bottles to their grandfather's thirsty players during practices.

It was one big sports event when Brees's family got together. They played basketball, football, and Wiffle ball well into the night. And they spit plum pits!

Drew has a large birthmark on his cheek. His parents told him it was left by angels that kissed him there. But his classmates teased him about it. Drew could have had the birthmark removed but did not. He decided that it made him unique.

Drew was a great athlete by the time he went to Westlake High School in 1993. But he wanted to play college baseball, not football. He nearly quit football. He thought he would never get the chance to play quarterback. But then Westlake's starting quarterback got hurt. Drew got his chance, and he ran with it. He led the football team to an undefeated season during his junior year.

Soon Drew began receiving letters of interest from college football coaches. But after he hurt his knee during the high school playoffs, the letters stopped. He still wanted to get a baseball scholarship for college, too. But his future in both sports seemed to be fading away.

Drew felt that his athletic career was over. However, he didn't quit playing. Instead, he worked hard to strengthen his knee. Drew didn't regret his hard work. He played football again

Drew has worked hard and overcome many obstacles in his path to become an NFL star.

during his senior year. He led Westlake to the state title. Drew threw for 31 touchdowns and was honored as Texas's Most Valuable Player (MVP). Westlake won all 28 of the games that Drew started at quarterback in his career.

Some colleges began showing interest in Drew again. Soon, he decided to focus on playing college football instead of baseball. He chose to play for Purdue University in Indiana.

Drew Brees

CHAPTER 2

BECOMING A STAR

Many great quarterbacks have played for Purdue University's football team, the Boilermakers. Among them are Pro Football Hall of Fame players Len Dawson and Bob Griese. Drew Brees continued that tradition when he joined the team in 1997.

Brees showed great talent from the start. He even played in seven games during his freshman year. Very few freshmen get a chance to play in college football.

Brees became the next great quarterback to play for Purdue University.

Brees was one of the top quarterbacks in all of college football while at Purdue.

Brees became the Boilermakers' starting quarterback in 1998. He quickly showed he was one of the best players in college football. He was the Big Ten Conference Offensive Player of the Year. He also broke league and school records for completed passes (361), total passing yards (3,983), and passes for touchdowns (39). Brees impressed the college football world by passing for six touchdowns in one game. Then he did it again.

Purdue played Kansas State in the season-ending Alamo Bowl. Brees threw for three touchdowns in that game. The third touchdown gave Purdue the win with less than 30 seconds left.

Brees was just warming up. As a junior in 1999, he threw 25 touchdown passes. He also cut his interceptions from 20 to 12. Perhaps his best game was against Michigan State. Brees completed 40 passes for 509 yards and five touchdowns.

Brees was named Big Ten Conference Player of the Week eight times during his college career. That matched the record set by University of Wisconsin running back Ron Dayne.

Players can enter the NFL Draft after three years in college. Many people thought Brees would be a high draft pick if he entered the NFL Draft. But he decided to finish college and returned to Purdue for his senior year.

It was a busy time for Brees. In addition to playing football, he also volunteered at several charities. He took part in the Purdue Gentle Giants program. It helps elementary school students in the Purdue area. He also teamed up with the American Lung Association. He helped launch an antismoking program called "Enjoy the Brees."

Brees was involved with other charities, too. They included the March of Dimes, the Muscular Dystrophy Association, the Boys and Girls Club, and the Boy Scouts of America. Brees was also named the first winner of the Socrates Award. It's given each year to a college athlete who shows excellence in athletics, academics, and community service.

Brees's senior season at Purdue was great, too. He threw for 3,668 yards and 26 touchdowns. He was again chosen as the Big Ten's best player. Brees also won the Maxwell Award. It's given to the top college football player in the United States.

Brees's success helped Purdue have an excellent season. The Boilermakers won the Big Ten title. That earned them their

Purdue teammates Montrell Lowe, *left*, and Brees celebrate after Purdue earned a berth in the 2000 Rose Bowl.

first trip to the Rose Bowl in 34 years. The Rose Bowl is the oldest college football bowl game in the country.

Many people praised Brees for his football skills in college. But perhaps the highest praise came from a second-grade teacher. She spoke about Brees's positive influence on her students and his willingness to work with them one on one. She added that Brees had a heart bigger than the state of Texas.

Drew Brees

CHAPTER 3

ON TO THE CHARGERS

Drew Brees was raised in Texas. Then he played college football in Indiana. After that, he headed to Southern California. The San Diego Chargers selected Brees in the second round of the 2001 NFL Draft.

Some teams thought Brees was too short to play quarterback in the NFL. He was only 6 feet tall. But the Chargers had faith in him. And they needed a good quarterback. They had won only one game in 2000.

Brees performed well early on with the Chargers, but his team struggled to win games.

Two of Brees's childhood heroes were NFL quarterbacks Joe Montana and Drew Bledsoe. Montana was one of the greatest quarterbacks in league history. But why did Brees like Bledsoe, who was a good quarterback, but not a great one? Brees liked Bledsoe because they both had the same first name.

Few rookie quarterbacks are starting players in the NFL. Brees didn't start for the Chargers. He threw just 27 passes that season. He spent most of his time adjusting to the NFL. But he improved enough to be named the team's starter in 2002.

Brees performed well in his first season as the Chargers' starting quarterback. He threw for 3,284 yards and 17 touchdowns. But the next season he also discovered how hard it is to win in the NFL. The Chargers won only two of the 11 games in which Brees started. This was the first time that Brees wasn't leading a winning team. He was even benched for a time while the Chargers tried 41-year-old Doug Flutie as quarterback.

This was a tough time for Brees. He worked hard to improve on the field. But this was his worst period as an NFL quarterback.

The Chargers had two good quarterbacks in Philip Rivers, *left*, and Brees beginning in 2004.

The Chargers weren't sure if Brees would ever lead them to success. So they acquired another young quarterback named Philip Rivers in 2004. It was a challenging time for Brees.

However, he was thinking about more than football. He also thought about people who were in need. In 2003, he started the Brees Dream Foundation. The foundation has since helped earn more than $5 million for various causes. It has

Brees threw for 24 touchdowns in 2005, but he also threw 15 interceptions as the Chargers went 9–7.

helped fund cancer research. It has also helped rebuild schools, parks, and playgrounds in New Orleans and San Diego.

In 2004, Brees improved in nearly every way. He threw 27 touchdown passes and only seven interceptions. He was named the NFL Comeback Player of the Year. He was also voted into the Pro Bowl as one of the NFL's best players. Brees led the Chargers to the playoffs, but they lost in the first round.

The Chargers didn't know what to do. Brees had become one of the finest quarterbacks in the NFL. But Rivers seemed ready to play, too. The 2005 season didn't go very well for Brees and the Chargers. They had a winning record but missed the playoffs. Brees also hurt his right shoulder during the final game of the season.

The Chargers didn't know if Brees would ever play well again. They offered to pay him less money than he thought he was worth. Brees knew he didn't have to stay with the Chargers. He was a free agent. That meant he could play for any team in the NFL.

Brees decided it was time to leave San Diego. He went to New Orleans to play for the Saints. He would soon have a bigger effect on that city than he ever could have imagined.

Brees graduated from Purdue University in 2001. But he's still involved in the community of West Lafayette, Indiana, the home of Purdue. The Brees Dream Foundation puts on an annual golf tournament there to raise money to help youth in need.

Drew Brees

CHAPTER 4

SUPER BREES, SUPER BOWL

The city of New Orleans was in despair when Drew Brees came to town. Hurricane Katrina had pounded the city only a few months before. Hundreds of people were dead and thousands were homeless. The flooding had affected nearly everyone in Louisiana's largest city.

The Saints were in bad shape, too. They had been one of the worst teams in NFL history. And they were coming off a 3–13 season when Brees arrived.

Brees went about turning the Saints into a Super Bowl contender when he arrived in 2006.

The new quarterback clearly had a big job ahead of him. The people in his new city needed to hear some good news. Brees knew that he could use his money and fame to help fix the damage from the hurricane. And he learned that the Saints were really important to the city. So he also set out to improve his new city by improving his new team.

A HELPING HAND

Brees brought nearly $2 million to the Hurricane Katrina relief effort through his Rebuilding Dreams campaign.

Brees toured New Orleans after arriving in 2006. He was stunned by the damage done by the hurricane. He offered his help in many ways. The hurricane had destroyed the entire athletic center at Lusher Charter School. Brees's Rebuilding Dreams charity raised $671,000 to rebuild the center. Brees also launched the Quarterback Club. It brought together some of the city's wealthiest citizens to head up new projects. These

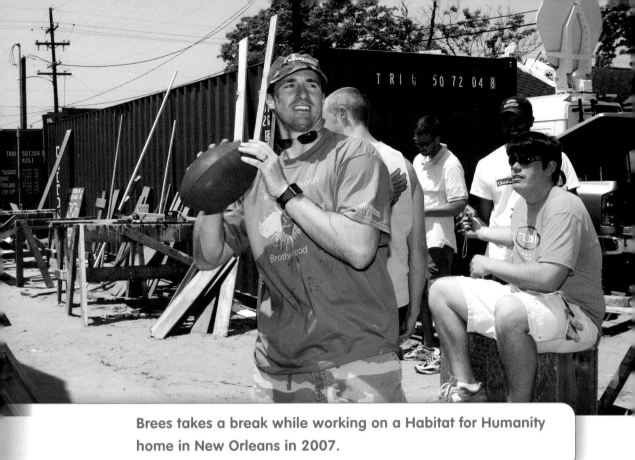

Brees takes a break while working on a Habitat for Humanity home in New Orleans in 2007.

people raised money for the New Orleans Ballet Association and the rebuilding of a stadium at City Park.

Saints fans had more to cheer about than Brees's charity. He was back in top playing form during the 2006 season. He threw for 26 touchdowns and led the NFL with 4,418 passing yards. With Brees as quarterback, the Saints were the most improved team in the league. They finished with a 10–6 record.

Brees led the Saints to the NFL's highest scoring offense in 2009. They averaged nearly 32 points per game.

They also made it to the playoffs for the first time in six years. The Saints' winning also helped renew a sense of pride and hope among the people of New Orleans.

Brees continued to improve. He had excellent passing records in 2007 and 2008. He was even the Offensive Player of the Year in 2008. However, the Saints had only average success those years. They missed the playoffs both times. But the team and the city were on the verge of something special.

In 2009, the Saints won their first 13 games. They had one of the greatest offenses in NFL history. Brees led the way. He set an NFL record by completing almost 71 percent of his passes. And he led the NFL again in touchdown passes. Even so, the Saints lost their last three games of the season.

Some fans were worried as the team headed into the playoffs. The Saints didn't disappoint them. They beat the Arizona Cardinals and the Minnesota Vikings in the playoffs. Brees threw six touchdown passes and no interceptions during these wins. The Saints reached the Super Bowl for the first time.

The people of New Orleans were thrilled! They were still recovering from Hurricane Katrina. But the Saints had brought them together.

At Purdue, Brees began dating a fellow student named Brittany. The two got married several years later, in 2003. On January 15, 2009, their son Baylen was born. He was born on Drew's thirtieth birthday. A year later, Drew lifted Baylen into the air as he and his teammates celebrated their Super Bowl win on the field.

Brees didn't let them down. The Saints played the Indianapolis Colts in the Super Bowl. The Colts featured star quarterback Peyton Manning. But Brees was the game's biggest star. He completed 32 of 39 passes for 288 yards and two touchdowns. He was chosen as the game's MVP. The Saints beat the Colts 31–17. The struggling city finally had something to celebrate.

Brees was a hero in New Orleans. But he wasn't just a hero for leading the Saints to an NFL championship. He was also a hero for helping the city recover from its worst tragedy ever. With Drew Brees leading the way, the people of New Orleans again had reason to be excited about their football team—and their city.

Brees and his son Baylen celebrate the Saints' victory in Super Bowl XLIV.

FUN FACTS AND QUOTES

- One of the sports that Drew Brees excelled in was tennis. At age 12, he was the top-ranked player in Texas. Among his early rivals was Andy Roddick. Roddick went on to become one of the top tennis players in the world.

- Drew and Brittany Brees love to visit other parts of the world. They have traveled to countries such as Croatia, Greece, and Australia. They have also visited Tahiti and the continent of Africa.

- Brees didn't follow his dream to play college baseball, but his brother did. Reid Brees earned a scholarship to play baseball at Baylor University. He helped his team reach the College World Series.

- Brees was an excellent student at Purdue. His grades continued to improve throughout college. He earned a perfect 4.0 grade point average (GPA) during the 2000 spring semester. He had a 3.4 GPA overall. Brees graduated in 2001 with a degree in industrial management.

- Nobody can be perfect, but Brees tries to be on the field. "I really think I ought to complete every pass," he said. "I don't think there's any reason I shouldn't. . . . By having that goal it makes me a better player."

WEB LINKS

To learn more about Drew Brees, visit ABDO Publishing Company online at **www.abdopublishing.com**. Web sites about Brees are featured on our Book Links page. These links are routinely monitored and updated to provide the most current information available.

GLOSSARY

charity
Money given or work done to help people in need.

despair
A feeling of hopelessness.

free agent
A player who is not under contract and who is allowed to sign with any team.

interception
In football, a pass thrown to a teammate but caught by someone on the opposing team.

launch
To begin something.

offense
The players on a football team who control the ball and try to score points.

playoffs
A series of games played after the regular season to determine which teams should go on to the Super Bowl.

quarterback
In football, the player who directs the team's offensive play.

scholarship
Money for tuition and other expenses given to a student by a college or other organization; often given to an outstanding athlete.

touchdown
In football, a six-point score that results when a player crosses the opponent's goal line with the ball.

INDEX

FURTHER RESOURCES

Brees, Drew. *Coming Back Stronger: Unleashing the Hidden Power of Adversity.*
    Carol Stream, IL: Tyndale House, 2010.

Fathow, Dan. *The New Orleans Saints Story: The 43-Year Road to the Super Bowl
    XLIV Championship.* New Orleans: Megalodon Entertainment, 2010.

Sandler, Michael. *Drew Brees and the New Orleans Saints: Super Bowl XLIV.* New
    York: Bearport, 2010.